Will You Ever Realise

DR SAKET SOURAV

First Published in April 2023

ISBN: 978-93-5628-270-4

BLUEROSE PUBLISHERS

www.BlueRoseONE.com

info@bluerosepublishers.com

+91 8882 898 898

Cover Design:

Aman Sharma

Typographic Design:

Namrata Saini

Distributed by: BlueRose, Amazon, Flipkart

Table of Contents

1.

Feeling Alone Even In A Crowded Place

Subham knew he would find it difficult to adjust in the big city, but thinking about getting admission in such a prestigious medical college in Mumbai ,after clearing all India medical entrance examination bring back a smile to his face., which he probably lost while chasing his dream to become a doctor

His main problem was that he was not accustomed to the city life, and as he was from government school, his English-speaking abilities were not good enough. His batchmates spoke in English all the time, so it was difficult for him to be part of their group in the medical college.

His other problem was that he has never studied in a co-education system, and so interacting with his female batchmates, especially regarding studies, was a difficult task for him.

Basically, he felt alone in the crowded place, a medical college that had a hundred students in each batch.

But with time, he got some so-called friends who actually enjoyed his innocence, and even after knowing all these, that they make joke of him Subham tried to be a part of their group as surviving alone in that place was difficult.

In his batch of one hundred students, 40 were girls. The lectures were held together, but for tutorials and practical classes, the students were divided into five groups of 20 each, and each group was arranged in an alphabetical order according to the name of students.

In Subham's group, there were 12 girls; As all their names started with 'S'.

Among them was Sandhya, who was a real combination of beauty and brain. Now every evening, whenever Subham got out of his hostel room to have evening snacks ,he had been asked to tell what Sandhya talked about or did in their tutorials as they wait for gossip outside his room...he tried to avoid to talk about them., but this was the only topic on which his Batch matess talk to him...

So he continued...

Actually in the tutorials, interactions among students were more frequent as they are fewer in numbers.

Actually, he also liked Sandhya, but he didn't want to make enemies out of everyone for liking her,

So he didn't even look at her.

Subham would tell everything in an exaggerated form, adding all kinds of spice to his stories so that everyone listens to him carefully, and after listening to his stories, someone would almost always ask Subham to have a cup of coffee and snacks with him. Subham would then smile, knowing that the particular guy just wanted more spice.

2.

The First Close Encounter

One day, in his practical classes, Arpita, who was allocated in group A, came forward and asked their teacher, 'Can I join this group for practical classes for few weeks?'

'Why?' their professor asked.

'Actually, Sir,' she replied, 'because of my mother's poor health, I missed some of the classes, and I want to make up for them through this group.'

'You can,' their professor said, 'if someone agrees to share their instruments and chemicals with you.'

There was complete silence in the room as no one wants to share their study material.

'Subham,' the professor interfered, 'do you have any problem with sharing with Arpita?'

‘No, sir’, he said, and so Arpita joined Subham. She was a classy girl; be it her looks or her way of talking, everything about her was impressive. She was quite intelligent too.

He was this close to a female batchmate for the first time, and this made him more nervous and cautious than usual; he was already thinking about how he has to tell an additional story today at his hostel.

Arpita came up to Subham and said, ‘Hello!’

‘Hi’, he replied softly. He felt as if his heart rate was going to surpass the upper normal limit.

‘Should we begin the test, then?’ Arpita asked.

‘Yes. Why don’t you proceed?’

‘Are you sure about giving it to me?

‘Yes’ Subham replied.

Actually., Glass slides were prepared by pricking one’s own fingers for a drop of blood, spreading it over the glass slide, and then, adding certain chemicals to it. The slide is then examined under the microscope.

As finger has to be pricked at first, and no one wants that. Arpita looked at Subham.

‘Do it,’ he said, ‘it’s all yours.’

'This time I want you to perform,' she said. 'I will do it later and just learn from the slide prepared by you now.'

'Don't worry,' he replied, 'it will not hurt you.' Saying this, he pricked her finger and took out a drop of blood on the glass slide, asking her to do the rest.

Arpita looked at Subham with tears in her eyes. Subham wondered if he had committed a crime. He consoled her, saying 'You are brave enough! Just do the job.'

Practically speaking, it is not easy to make a slide in the first attempt itself. Arpita was unable to do it and so her drop of blood was wasted. So they had to start it again.

'You are very strong,' Subham told her, 'give me your fingertip and I will prick it again.'

'No, Subham! It's your turn now.'

Subham realised there is no way out now and he asked Arpita to prick his finger as he can't do it himself.

'Sorry,' she said, 'I can't, I am not like you. Just do it on your own.'

Subham then exclaimed, 'Look what Sandhya is doing!' She turned to look at her, and when she had her eyes on Sandhya, he pricked himself and got a drop of blood on the slides.

'You did it!' Arpita said, but then saw Subham's fingertips continue to bleed, and so hurriedly held her finger to his and applied pressure over the point to stop the bleeding. 'How deep did you prick yourself?!'

'What could I do?' Subham shrugged. 'This is the last time anyway and I didn't want that both of us fail, so I pricked myself a little deep.'

She interrupted and said, 'And you distracted me and made me look the other way just to hide your pain.'

'Have you not seen Mr Amitabh Bachchan's movie called *MARD*?' Subham said, 'There was a famous dialogue that goes "*mard ko dard nahi hota*"' in the movie.' Both of them smiled at each other, now Subham was comfortable enough with her.

The slides had dried by then so he added the required chemicals to that and put it under the microscope. It actually turned out pretty good. He then took out another slide and added some chemicals to it.

'Where did the second slide come from?' Arpita asked.

'Actually, I prepared two. One for myself and the other one for you,' Subham replied. 'Now look at your slide under the microscope'

'Beautiful,' she said, looking into the microscope.

Till then the professor reached Subham. He was annoyed as none of the students had done it properly but after seeing Subham's slide, he complimented him, saying 'You have done a very good job.'

Subham then moved the second slide under the microscope and said, 'That's Arpita's slide, please take a look at it.'

'Beautiful,' said the professor after looking at the slide.

The professor turned to Arpita. 'Why you are holding Subham's finger?'

'Actually, sir,' she said, 'he was bleeding through it.'

'Okay but leave it now, otherwise there will be a different kind of problem.'

The whole lab laughed and she looked at Subham with angry eyes. Subham looked back at her innocently and said, 'I didn't do anything.'

But his finger was still bleeding so he himself pressed on it and after class, put a Handiplast on it.

The next day, anatomy tutorials were on routines. Subham was asked to work on the right upper limb and was grouped with four other boys. The task of dividing the 20 students into groups was given to him by the professor, so he put only boys in his group and mixed the rest of the students.

Dissection was going on when one boy from Subham's group turned to him. 'We know that you are a *brahmchari* but why do you have to drag us down with you? I am going to work with the other groups. You can be alone if you want to'. Within five minutes, Subham found himself alone as the rest of the boys from his group join other groups with girls.

The professor will come after an hour to check on the task and now he alone will have to complete it himself. So he started and did the job by himself.

From the rest of the tables, Subham could hear high-quality discussions going on regarding things that were beyond Subham's knowledge.

Soon the professor come to check on them. 'You all have done good,' he said. Then he saw Subham and asked, 'Why are you alone?'

'Don't know sir, where rest of my Bachmets had gone,' Subham said slowly.

'Okay, let me check,' the professor said and then discussed the anatomy dissection Subham did.

At last he said 'Before leaving the class, everyone had to see it. It's a must, it is done beautifully!'

Sandhya came up to Subham and asked him to explain it to her but he didn't respond, as he sensed lots of angry eyes are looking at him

'Hello! I am talking to you,' she said.

'Yeah, I know' he replied. He then explained things in brief and told her that he has some urgent work right now so he needs to leave for that, 'You are intelligent enough so you can probably understand the rest of the things by yourself.'

In the evening, as he came out of his hostel room, a few seniors were waiting for him in the balcony

Subham greeted him. He asked Subham how it was going. 'Good, boss,' he replied.

'So, we heard that all the Miss Indias of your batch are involved with you'

'No, boss. That was just a coincidence.'

'Keep a minimum distance of 5 feet between them and you, understand?' They told him in strict voice.

'Yes, boss,' Subham replied.

In medical colleges, seniors are honoured with the designation of 'boss' and the concept was that the 'boss' is always right.

'What are you thinking about?' One of his senior asked. 'Today you will have dinner with us outside, so now please smile.'

Subham smiled. Such was the beauty of medical fraternities. The juniors respected their seniors and the seniors treated them as their younger brothers, and it continues throughout their lives.

For the first time, he had dinner with his seniors. They talked a lot and told Subham, 'You are innocent; you don't understand a lot of the local things, especially things regarding girls, so it is better for you to just concentrate on your studies and forget about them. We don't want to see you in trouble.'

3.

Trouble Started

But trouble had already started. Just after their lectures, Sandhya and Arpita stopped them.

'What?' he asked.

'We heard that you talk about us among the hostel boys,' Sandhya started, 'Don't try to act smart, which we all know you are not, and stop these activities immediately.'

After a pause Subham asked Arpita, 'Do you also want to say something?'

She was surprised by the question and shook her head to say no.

'Look, Sandhya,' Subham said, 'I don't know what you heard But believe me , I never talked with wrong intentions regarding both of you but yes I talked and I regret my act but I promise as part of my regret to both of you that you won't see me unless you turned around in search of me.

Is that okay?'

Yes that's better...and don't dare to repeat this kind of act.

Subham nodded his head in yes and left

The boys were laughing as they now had a new topic to discuss among themselves. Subham had been scolded in front of the whole batch by two of the girls of their batch!

Subham came to his room. He wanted to cry as he had to hear a lot in front of his whole batch and now all of his Batch matess will create mess of him.

He missed all his classes that day.

The next day, he requested the Principal of the college to change his tutorial group to A. The principal asked him the reason, but he didn't reply.

'Okay, my boy,' he said, 'from today onwards, you will be in group A and Arpita will replace you in group E.'

Now Subham Started to sat at the last bench of their lecture theatre,to hide himself.

He left all his so-called friends behind, concentrated solely on his studies and started to take things sportingly. If someone ask him what Sandhya had said while scolding him, he started telling that she scolded me with all the terrible words you could think of in the world.

'And you just listened to it and didn't respond?' they would ask.

'No,' he would reply, 'I am a coward. Her words terrified me and I quit from there.' After that, he would laugh. Gradually, people stopped asking him these questions.

The next day, in the pathology lab tutorial, the professor asked where Subham was. Nobody answered, so the professor asked Arpita.

'His tutorial place was replaced with mine as per his request,' she informed the professor, 'he is now in group A.'

Truthfully, Arpita was missing him and even felt guilty for her behaviour towards him. Repeatedly asking why see came in talks of Sandhya, and hurt an innocent boy.

Subham, however, with only boys in his group, was much more comfortable now. And the best part was that now he didn't have to tell anyone any stories about Sandhya and Arpita.

One day, while walking on the main road, he saw a small crowd. He went there and found Sandhya was injured; her Scooty skid on the main road. He came forward to straighten the Scooty and helped her stand up, telling her to calm down as everything is okay.

Subham started the Scooty and ask her to sit but she was not able to do so. He applied the centre stand of the Scooty and lifted her up, helping her sit on the Scooty.

'Are you okay?' he asked her. She nodded her head and said yes. He drove her to an emergency department, where he handed her over to the professor for treatment, and gave her the keys to the Scooty. 'Don't let anybody know that I was with you,' he told her gently, 'take care.'

After 3 weeks she was almost fully recovered.

4.

Now She Asked For Coffee

The very next day, she asked Subham to have a cup of coffee with her outside their campus.

'What?' he asked.

She repeated the words again.

Subham went on his first date with her to a coffee house. She thanked him and said, 'You probably faced some problems because of me.'

'It's okay,' Subham said, 'it was only because of your weight that I developed back pain after lifting you!'

'Listen here, my weight is fine!'

'Then I must practice lifting girls to avoid such problems.'

They both laughed.

After casually talking for a long time, they left.

But you can't hide anything in medical colleges. This act of Subham spread like wildfire in their campus. All the things were explained in a much aggravated manner.'

Some said Subham actually saved Sandhya's life while others said Subham carried her in his arms after her major accident.

Some of his batchmates told him that Sandhya was in search of him. Some told him she had actually fallen in love with him. Listening to all these 24 hours a day made him make a space inside him for Sandhya. He started dreaming of being with her. He would have a smile on his face just by thinking about her. He thought a lot about their talks at the coffee house. He felt a new kind of emotional energy inside him.

He now went to all his lectures well dressed, left all his casual activities that girls do not like behind him.

One day, while entering his tutorial class, they came face-to-face. Both of them tried to give the other space to move on but both of them did it at the same time, which resulted in both facing each other for more than five minutes.

Suddenly, they heard the professor's voice and moved apart.

Such episodes made Subham's days beautiful.

Sandhya smiling at him just once made his entire day, and he waited for that everyday.

Valentine's Day was close and he had everything planned. However, one day, while coming out of the lecture theatre, he heard some boys and girls planning for a party tonight. Sandhya was one of them.

Some of them asked if they can invite Subham along but Sandhya said, 'Oh no, not again! He is so boring. He is not even from our class so don't even think about including him with us!'

5.

Heart Break

Subham heard every word of that and felt a deep-seated pain inside him, as if someone had put a knife inside him, but just he moved on through the exit door to the other side.

He entered his hostel room and looked around.

He felt completely shattered. He tore up the Valentine's Day card which he had bought for her. He couldn't hold in his emotions and they came out as tears. But he just took out his books for the next lecture and moved towards the lecture theatre.

Upon entering the lecture theatre, he found just two students inside. Sandhya and Arpita.

He instantly moved out of the lecture theatre and stood outside in the balcony.

'Hello, Subham.' It was Sandhya's voice.

Subham directly asked her what she wanted.

She was a bit surprised by his cold response.

'How are you?' she asked.

'Fine, thank you.'

'Are you alright?' Sandhya asked.

'Yes, I am alright as now I know I don't match the class of you belong to.'

'Hey, I just said that to protect you from the night party as I don't like those and I didn't want to involve you with them.'

'Anyway,' Subham said, 'keep a distance of at least 5 feet from me while we talk.'

'What?'

'Yes, this is an order from my seniors.'

'Why?'

'I don't know, maybe some of them like you and don't want to see me talking to you.'

'All these are rubbish. We are just friends.'

'Madam, in general, concept is a bit different. A boy and a girl cannot be just friends.'

'I don't care, you are my friend.'

'But I am not yours, as I am boring and not smart enough to be with you.'

'Now, don't take my words seriously, as now I understand the situation clearly.'

'What clearly? I hope there is some misunderstanding.'

'Look Subham, you are a good guy but I want to make it clear that there is nothing from my side.'

'I know that,' he said, 'Now, will you please smile?' Subham replied.

'Why?'

'Because when you smile, the dimple in your cheek looks beautiful.'

She smiled.

Subham moved out of the talk by diverting her mind and left.

She said goodbye, but Subham didn't respond. She didn't like him, it was clear now, yet he was unable to get her out of his thoughts. *When she clearly didn't like me, why am I unable to get over her thought*, he repeatedly asked to himself.

The irony of all these self-question was that the more he wanted to get away from her, the more she came into his thoughts. He accumulated the torn pieces of the Valentine's Day card and tried to glue them back together. He wanted to keep it with him as a lesson. He didn't know what he can do to get her out of his thoughts. He was really disturbed and wanted to get out of it anyhow.

6.

Why I Loved

But it's not easy, he realized that.

And asked himself, *why did I love?*

The most problematic thing was his hostel neighbours who constantly asked him about Sandhya to tease him.

Initially, he avoided them but he could not get rid of them. So one day, he declared that Sandhya dumped him. The news spread like wildfire in the campus. Now people started saying that there was once an affair between them but she dumped him later. But at least, Subham got relief from the repeated questions regarding Sandhya.

Subham searched for a place in the garden near the hospital where he started sitting in with his books for study. The best thing was that there was no one there to ask him any questions like in his hostel. He can't even go to the library as he has to face Sandhya there. So now his routine included reaching that place by 5pm and studying there till 9:30 pm at least.

One evening, he heard hello. He turned around and saw Arpita. He didn't responded.

'What are you doing here?' she asked him.

'I should be asking you this as I come here daily,' Subham replied.

'I just came from behind you.'

'Why?'

'I don't need your permission to do that.'

Subham didn't respond to that.

'Why are you annoyed with me?' Arpita asked.

'I am not annoyed with anyone,' Subham replied, 'kindly just leave me alone.'

'I can't leave such a cute boy alone.'

Subham smiled. 'Are you flirting with me?'

'You can think that. It doesn't really matter to me.'

'Okay, just keep a distance of 5 feet from me. I don't want to disobey my seniors,' Subham said.

'I heard that Sandhya dumped you as you don't belong to her class.'

'Yes.'

'Can you tell me which class you are presently in?'

'Nursery,' he replied, 'can you leave me alone now?'

'Do you know, even if you don't speak, your eyes speak for you?'

'Hey, what do you want?'

'I want you to smile, like you used to in the lab with me in the initial days.'

'Do you know, you lost it.'

7.

Do You Know You Lost Your Smile

Subham hid his eyes with his arm. Arpita wanted to come close to him but he stopped her by telling her that he had something in his eyes. In realty, he was just trying to hide his tears, and Arpita could sense that.

'Are you ok?' she asked him.

'Yes, I am trying to bring those things back, but I don't know when that will happen.'

'The truth is that there is no one in our batch who can match your class.'

'Oh really?'

'Yes and that is a fact. Fight back. Don't think that *she* dumped *you*. In fact, *she* is the one who lost *you*, and honestly speaking, I am jealous of her. Had I been in her place, I would never have allowed these tears to come through your eyes. They wouldn't even have dared to come out in my presence. But these things don't matter. I just want your smile back, and to stop feeling this way. The individual who is not with you whom you would have liked to be with you just missed a golden opportunity.'

These words touched inside Subham deeply. He stood up and came close to Arpita.

'Okay,' he said, 'I will do that. Thank you so much for being with me, I will not forget these words throughout my life.'

He then asked her to leave as the sun had started to set.

'Can we have coffee together?' she asked.

'Of course,' he replied, 'we will have it but some other day.'

He walk along with her till the streetlights were switched on and the roads were well-lighted, and watched her till she entered her hostel gate. She turned around and said bye to him. Subham just smiled and turned around.

After reaching his hostel room, he took a bath and looked himself in the mirror. He could feel the changes in himself since he heard those words from Sandhya.

After five minutes, he smiled and told himself that the game of life is still on and so he will play it beautifully.

The next day, while he was going for his tutorial classes upstairs, he found Sandhya and Arpita, along with some other students, coming downstairs as their tutorials had just finished.

But this time, Subham didn't change the route. Suddenly Sandhya slipped from stairs, but Subham saved her from getting injured by holding her arms firmly. She looked at Subham with a sense of gratitude for saving her.

'Be careful,' Subham said, 'And moved upstairs.'

All his batchmates were surprised by his bold behaviour. After reaching the upper floor, Subham turned around. 'Arpita?'

'Yes?' She was surprised and felt awkward in front of her batchmates.

He asked her in slow voice.

'Did you look at yourself in the mirror today?' Subham asked.

'What?'

'I asked if you looked at yourself in the mirror today.'

'Yes.' She was a bit uncomfortable but replied anyway.

'He told., you didn't even notice that you had an earring only on one side.'

She touched her ears and found this to be true. But till then, Subham had already moved inside the class. She was really surprised to see that kind of self-confidence in Subham.

At the end of the day, when classes were over, Subham found Arpita with Sandhya on their way back.

'Can I have a few seconds of your time?' he asked Arpita.

She felt uncomfortable and asked, 'Why?'

Subham moved towards her and said, 'He held her hand, put something against her palm and left.

'He is really rude,' Sandhya said. Arpita didn't respond.

Even after Sandhya repeatedly asking her what he put in her hands, Arpita didn't answer. She was completely surprised. 'I will let you know once I open the envelope.'

But Sandhya insisted Arpita to open the envelope, telling her that they could complain against him if something wrong found in the envelope.

'Please don't you worry,' Arpita said, 'I am confident enough to handle any misbehaviour. And I trust Subham, he won't do anything wrong.'

Finally she opened the envelope, with beside her. There was a small box inside.

On opening the box, both of them where surprised to find Arpita's missing earring inside. Arpita took it out and looked at it for few seconds, smiling shyly.

'He is a good guy,' she said. 'A really good guy.' Saying this, she ran towards her room.

Sandhya came into her room two hours later and found her still watching the earrings.

'Have you gone mad?' she asked.

When Arpita heard her voice, she tried to hide the earring.

'What were you doing?' Sandhya asked her. 'And how did your earrings reach him?'

'I was with him last evening'. May be it had lost there

She smiled and looked at the earring.

'Are you okay? What are you saying?' Sandhya asked.

'Yeah, I am telling the truth.'

'Do you like him?' Sandhya enquired

'Yes, of course.'

'He is not of our class.'

‘I asked him about his class. He said he is in nursery right know, so I also took admission in nursery,’ said Arpita. ‘By the way, I hope you don’t have any problem with us.’

‘No, of course not.’

‘Then why did the colour of on face suddenly fade away?’

Sandhya instantly left the room.

Now after few days there examination for first year MBBS started..

Which continued for around a month and now post exam vacation was declared...

The trip of a lifetime...

Tomorrow morning, the whole batch was going to Goa for a trip as post exam vacation started initially when it was planned Subham didn’t want to go because of Sandhya.

One of the professors of administrative posts was also with them to regulate the trip. He checked the attendance of all the students and asked where Subham was. The monitoring committee of students informed him that Subham did not want to go on the trip as he didn’t want to waste any money.

'Call him immediately and tell him that I am bearing all his expenses. Convey it to him to take this as an order and that he only has ten minutes in his hands.'

'Within seven minutes,' Subham was in front of the professor.

'Good morning, sir.'

'Where is your luggage?'

'I didn't bring anything as they told me that you will purchase the things for me, Sir.'

The professor looked at him and smiled.

'Don't you worry, sir. I brought everything with me,' Subham said.

The professor just held his ears with love. 'You are like my son. You just lost your chance, otherwise you would've had a whole new set of clothes. Come, sit. We are getting late.'

Right when the professor asked if there was anyone left, Sandhya reached the stairs of the bus in a hurry and almost fell down, but someone held her.

'Oh god,' she said and then moved inside the bus, holding onto the hand supporting her.

'Now kindly leave my hands.'

'Oh. Sure.'

She saw it was Subham. Peoples started laughing.

Subham sat down on his seat near the window after few minutes he felt someone sitting on his nearby seat...

'*Aagaye*?' he asked her.

'How did you know it was me without seeing?'

No other sit was empty.

'Ask Arpita to sit with me,' he said, 'you'll be more comfortable at her place as it is a long journey of around ten hours. Please don't you worry about my comfort.'

'If you have a problem, go and sit by her side,' she retorted.

'I don't have any problem. Today you probably applied high-class deodorant any way.'

'And you had applied nursery class deo, right?'

'Ooh so you know my class! That's really good.'

After few minutes of silence, Subham turned to Sandhya. 'Why have you been looking at me for so long?'

She just turned around. 'Why will I look at you? Why would you say that?'

'It's quite simple, mam the selfie mode of my mobile is on and I saw you in that.'

For the first time, Sandhya smiled. 'Keep smiling,' Subham said, 'it looks good.'

'And why did you open the selfie mode of your mobile? To look at me?' asked Sandhya.

'No, madam. Actually, in a hurry, I didn't look at myself at the mirror,' he replied.

'Now, why would you care about your looks?'

He smiled but didn't reply, so she asked again.

'Actually, not everyone is like you. There may be someone here who might want to have a look at me. This is why I care. Anything else you want to ask?'

'No.'

Subham leaned on the bus' window. Sandhya searched for something in her purse and after not finding it, looked disappointed. Subham looked over at her and offered her his headphones. She looked surprised.

'How did you know I was searching for that?'

'Take mine. Return them to me after the trip,' he told her.

'But how did you know?' she asked.

'It's simple. You had the music files on your phone opened.'

'Do you also happen to have a third eye?'

'No, it is just the art of understanding.'

Subham continued to lean on the glass. Sandhya listened to music with the headphones Subham gave her.

After few minutes, she turned to Subham. '*So rahe ho kya?*'

'Yes. Trying to, at least.'

'Why so early?'

'Didn't sleep last night. Had some pending work. You people will know about it in one of these days. You are not enjoying your music,' he pointed out. 'What do you want to do?'

'I want to talk to you but you are trying to sleep.'

'I am listening to you. I know you have thousands of questions inside you and I will reply till I fall asleep.'

'You have changed a lot.'

'When you lose all sorts of love, affection and expectations from someone, you will change. And so I changed.'

'Did you like me at some point?' Sandhya asked.

'Yes. And you made me cry. Then I learnt my lessons from that episode and changed myself.'

'You still have something for me inside you.'

'No, mam, you lost it.'

'Then for whom did you check your looks for?'

Subham didn't answer as he fell asleep.

Thirty minutes had passed by when the bus stopped at a place for breakfast but Subham still asleep. Sandhya came out of the bus and joined Arpita.

'So how is the trip going with Subham?' Arpita asked.

Sandhya didn't reply.

'If you feel uncomfortable there, you can come to my seat,' Arpita offered.

'No, Arpita. I am sorry. I want to be with him.'

'But what about your class?'

'I also took admission in nursery,' said Sandhya.

Both of them laughed.

'Are you jealous of me?' Sandhya asked Arpita.

'Yes,' she said, 'I wanted to be with him as talking to him gives me immense pleasure.

'Alright ...will think about that,' Sandhya replied and laughed

After returning to the seat, Sandhya found Subham is still sleeping and her seat being occupied by another boy.

'Leave my seat,' she told him.

'He said he had arranged your window-side seat with other girls. Go there, you will be far more comfortable.'

'I will sit here itself,' she told him. 'Go to your own place.'

Finally the professor interfered and asked, 'What happened?'

'Sandhya, do you have any problem sitting with Subham?'

'No,' she said. 'I want to seat in my own seat again.'

The professor then asked the monitoring group individuals to give her the seat back.

As that boy moved out, Sandhya occupied the seat next to Subham. Subham woke up and asked what the noise was about. Sandhya just told him to go back to sleep. 'It's only been an hour into the trip now and you have slept for 40 minutes already.'

'You are sitting by my side. I don't want anything else, so let me sleep,' he said.

She looked at him. There was a sweet smile on Subham's face. It seemed like he was aware of the dispute regarding the seat.

Subham sat back straight on his sit, took out his bag, and had some water from his bottle which he had kept inside his handbag. He took out his glasses and a suspense thriller book from his bag.

'You wear glasses?' Sandhya asked.

'Yes.'

'I have never seen you in them.'

He closed the book and turned to look at her. 'What? So that means you watch me daily.'

'No no, I never said that!'

'Actually, I don't like them, but now I start feeling a pain behind my eyes whenever I don't wear them, so I always try to wear it. In fact, it does not have much power, it's just for precautions.'

'Okay.'

'Which song are you listening to?' Subham asked.

She was silent for some moment and then named some Hollywood song Subham wasn't familiar with. Subham looked at her. 'You are lying.' He opened his book again.

'Why will I lie to you?'

'Because, mam' Subham pointed out, 'You forgot to tap on the play button on your phone screen, which I think is necessary to listen to any music.'

Sandhya was a bit uncomfortable and touched the play option, but soon paused it. She looked at Subham. He was again leaning on the glass of his window and appeared to be buried in some thoughts. 'What are you thinking about?'

'You are asking me?' he asked.

'Yeah, of course. There is no one else nearby.'

He smiled and turned towards her. 'I was thinking about what you are thinking about.'

'Do you always think about me?' Sandhya asked him.

'No. There was a time when I used to, but not anymore, not now.'

'Why?'

'Because I learn from my mistakes quickly and do not repeat them.'

'What did you realise about your mistakes?' she asked.

'Leave it, the matter is over with now.'

'No,' she said. 'I want to know.'

'Do you know?'

'What?'

'The fact is that you are enjoying talking to me,' Subham said.

'It doesn't matter what you think,' Sandhya said. 'Tell me what I had asked.'

'Look, don't take my words the wrong way. I don't want to have any arguments over this and no questions please, if you agree with that, only then I can tell you.'

'I accept your terms,' she said.

'Look, there were days when I really liked you. That lead to a lot of suffering for me. It was difficult for me to be in class or hostel as everyone around me wanted to tease me with your name. They enjoyed that. I couldn't even go to library because you were there all the time. Even you scolded me in front of everyone. Do you remember that?'

She didn't replied.

'After that you repeatedly talked regarding my class.'

This makes my situation even worse...

Somehow, I found a place where there was complete silence as there was no one there. After class, I started going to that place. In fact that place became my home. I just went to my hostel room at 11 pm to sleep after having dinner. The rest of the time, I was there. I even kept two bedsheets and a pillow there. There was a light there for me to study but not enough, and the glasses you see on me now is because of that. One day someone told me that I lost myself for you, and asked me to bring myself back.

That words impacted me deep inside.

There was a small pond near that place. I went to that pond to wash my face, while washing my face, I looked at the reflection of my face in pond. I continued to look at it for some time. I thought about what I did to myself, I asked myself how much I had deteriorated because of you. *What's going on,* I asked myself. *Why I am here and why I am trying to hide myself? I didn't commit any crime.* I washed my face repeatedly and asked myself, *how do I come out of all these as soon as possible?* I left all my study that evening .I wiped my face and asked myself who I am doing all these for. Then I began to remember your words. The only word which repeatedly came in my mind was your *class, class* and *class*... I began to think *why this class? What does it mean?* I arrived at the conclusion that the class which you told me about was different. You mean smartness by that. Style. Party. English speaking, and a lot of other things which belong to one's superficial appearance. I figured that the class difference between us was actually of thoughts regarding emotions. For you, superficial appearance is class. You do whatever you enjoy. You actually take things practically and emotions come last in the sequence of your decision making. For me, the list is in reverse. Emotions arc, in fact, one of the priority factors with any other practical factors in any work or any decision making. I can't go for something which practically is very good for me but can hurt anyone. I feel better about work which may not benefit me much but do not hurt anyone. When I understood all these, I left you, because I cannot be with a person who does not respect emotions. I was wasting my life for her. I don't remember after how many days I actually smiled; I was happy that night. someone asked me about my class. I said, 'nursery don't know that individual understands that concept or not...but I am and will be highly obliged to him till last.'

'Can you tell me why I said nursery?'

Sandhya didn't respond. She was completely lost.

'Hey, I am asking you.'

Somehow, she shook her head to say no.

'Because,' Subham continued, 'when you see the children of nursery class, you feel the purity of emotions in them. They do not think which work they will get more benefits from. They just like love and affection as they don't have any idea of the practical world. I was, and still am, the same. It is only my understanding of facts that improve my sufferings.'

Sandhya got up from her seat and went to Arpita. After a few seconds, Arpita came and sat by Subham's side.

'What did you say to her?' she asked Subham.

'Nothing serious.'

'Then why are her eyes wet?'

'I don't know.'

She asked me the same question again and again, and after repeated questions, I told her everything.

'I saw her in tears for the first time,' she said.

'Here is her phone, give it to her.' Till then, the bus had stopped for lunch. Subham came out of the bus.

'Why do the girls want to sit by your side?' his colleagues asked him. He told them a better reply will be given by the girls themselves and laughed.

After a good meal, Subham sat by the side of a tree. The natural air blowing through the place made it much better than the inside of the air-conditioned bus. Suddenly he heard the horn of the bus. He went back to his seat. He adjusted his seat as it was a sleeper coach, took out a thin blanket and lied down.

His adjoining seat was empty.

After about an hour, he felt a sudden pinch in his arm. He woke up with a start and looked at his arm. *What had happened?*

He looked at his adjoining sit. 'You came back again.' It was Sandhya.

'Yeah, it's my seat. Do you have any problem with that...' she trailed off as she saw that Subham had fallen asleep again.

A few minutes later, he woke up again as he felt a pinch again. Straightening his sit, he searched for some sort of insect or anything similar but couldn't find anything. He looked back at his arm, and then looked at Sandhya. She was busy reading his book.

He took a deep breath and straightened the book in her hand. 'Now read,' he said, 'it is very difficult to read a book upside-down. And yes, cut your nails short.'

She hid her face with the book. After a few seconds, she closed the book.

'You are fast enough. You completed it very fast.'

'No, I didn't.'

'Then do it.'

'No, I don't want to.'

'You want to read me. Yes or no?'

'Yes.'

'It's very difficult.'

She smiled. 'I am really sorry,' she said.

'You are disobeying the agreement we had earlier.'

'Yes, I know. But I want to say something.'

'Please don't.'

'The time will come when you will get the answers to the rest of your questions. But I may not be there to hear them, and you will search for me to tell me the answers.'

'Take some rest. You will feel better.'

She obeyed him, took out his blanket and lied down. It was actually really cold inside bus, so Subham also took his own blanket.

After about 15 minutes, he noticed that the whole bus was sleeping. Subham turned around and saw Arpita. She was trying to sleep but probably didn't bring a blanket with her and was feeling cold. Subham folded his blanket and slowly came out of his seat, trying not to disturb Sandhya. He moved towards Arpita and slowly covered her with a blanket. He returned to his seat, feeling quite cold himself. He took out another shirt of his and wore it over previous one. Sandhya couldn't hold back her smile as she saw all these.

Subham leaned against the glass window and looked outside.

8.

Self Realisation

The emotional aspect of the thoughts of Subham are, in reality, right in front of her. She tried to sleep but couldn't figure out where her sleep had gone. She closed her eyes.

After around 30 minutes, Subham woke up suddenly as he felt a few drops of water on his face. He saw Sandhya in front of him with a bottle of water in her hand.

'The bottle actually slipped and a few drops of water fell onto your face,' she told him. 'I am really sorry.'

Subham didn't say a word. He wiped his face and wore his glasses.

'Are you annoyed with me?'

He didn't reply again.

'Please say something.'

He took a long breath and asked, 'What do you want to hear?'

'Your voice,' Sandhya replied.

'You are already hearing it.'

'Don't sleep that much. You have been asleep for one and a half hours in the last four hours. Look, now only six hours are left after which we will reach Goa. And I don't know if I will have time over there for you or not. So you should talk to me as much as you can now as you may not get this golden opportunity again.'

Subham smiled and said, 'Yeah, you are right. Thanks for reminding me of this golden opportunity. You want to ask me something. You can ask.'

'Do you like Arpita?' Sandhya asked.

'I don't know.'

'Then why did you give her your blanket?'

Subham turned to her and said, 'You really are watching me every second. I thought you are sleeping.'

'No, I wasn't asleep at that time. Tell me. Why did you do that?'

'I would have done the same thing if it were you at her seat,' Subham replied. 'But yes, I do care for her. I saw a component of myself in her. I don't want to see her in any problem. Now next question please.'

'No further questions.'

'Do you remember how many times I saved you?'

'Many times, I think.'

'But Arpita never asked if I still like you or not. When you like someone, it does not matter if he or she is with you or not. You only want his or her smile. You should not try to possess them. So, now please smile.'

'That means you still like me,' Sandhya said.

'You can interpret it any way you want to.'

Sandhya smiled and pulled her blanket over her head. But within few seconds, she removed it.

'Don't worry,' Subham reassured her, 'I will not sleep again. Now why are you looking at me like this?

Don't tell me you have even more questions for me.'

'Yeah,' she said, 'I want to ask you something.'

'Hey, actually, I want to ask *you* something,' Subham said.

'Yes, of course. It would be a pleasure.'

'Be my roommate in Goa,' Subham told her. 'You will get enough time there to ask me your questions.'

'You try to portray yourself as an innocent individual but you are not.'

'I never told you that I am innocent! You interpreted it yourself, it's not my fault,' Subham replied and started laughing.

'Oh, it's nice to see you laughing.' It was Arpita.

'Hey.' Subham turned to look at her. 'How are you?'

'Fine. Not enjoying it as much as you guys, though. Why are you wearing two shirts?'

'It was cold so I wore two.'

'Did you not bring your blanket?' Arpita asked Subham.

He looked at Sandhya. 'No,' he said, 'I didn't.'

'How will you cope with the cold? During the evening, there will be a further fall in the temperature.'

'I will manage, I have a few more shirts.'

'You don't need to do that. Take back your blanket. I felt you covering me with it. Thanks for caring.'

'Keep it,' he said. 'I will manage.'

'Honestly speaking,' Arpita told him, 'I don't really want to return it to you. I want to keep it with me forever. But I can't see you in a problem.'

Sandhya, who was just looking at them the whole time, interfered. 'Look, Subham's blanket is longer. Give it back to Subham, we can share it. You can take mine.'

Arpita looked at Sandhya. 'No, it'd be better to have him in two or more shirts. You can keep your blanket to yourself, I will purchase him new one.'

A smile came over Sandhya's face, but after looking Subham, she became serious again. She was expecting Subham to also smile, but he was just lost in some thoughts, leaning against the glass of the window, looking outside. This time, she didn't disturb him and just continued to look at him.

In his glasses, he looked more thoughtful and gentle.

'Did you bring any *kajal*?' Subham asked her.

'No,' she said. 'Why do you need *kajal*?'

'To protect myself from your eye,' he replied. '*Are kahi nazar na lag jae humko*.'

She smiled at him and said, '*Aapno ki najar nahi lagti hai*.'

'*Accha tum kab se meri apni ho gaye?*'

'*Bas abhi se man lo*.'

Subham smiled. Sandhya continued, '*Itna pata hai dusman nahi huu mai tumhari*.'

'In fact,' Subham said, 'I am really thankful to you for all your rude remarks and behaviour in front of everyone, which actually made me a better individual now as, for the first time, I introspected myself.'

'Please leave that behind. Can we get a new start?'

'No, Sandhya. You are good, stay like this. People with emotional priority suffer a lot. I can't forget those things easily. You were asking about my suffering. Never. I don't know how many nights I didn't sleep, or how many days I skipped my meals. I forgot to smile because of you. You talked so rudely and loudly to me in front of everyone, and dishonoured me. I can't forget all that. It taught me things that are not written in any book.'

'Please. Forget all these.'

'No.'

'Okay. Then you can talk to me rudely in front of everyone. That way it will balance things out and we can move on.'

'I am not like you. I will think a hundred times before hurting anyone.'

'Then how do we neutralise it? I permit you to do anything with me, just please forgive me.'

'Hey, why are you so worried? I am still with you.'

'I know you are with me with all your old sufferings, which means we can't walk together too long.'

'Don't you worry so much,' Subham said. 'I will not be with all of you soon.'

'Why? Are you going to leave the college?'

'No. Have some patience, you all will know everything at the right time. Enjoy Goa. Enjoy your life. No one dies without anyone. So move on. Erase this ten-hour trip from your memory.'

'I can't. I will keep every second of it recorded and displayed in my mind.'

'Hey, look!' Subham exclaimed. 'Beaches! Look how beautiful they are!'

Sandhya's didn't reply.

'If someone made some mistakes in her life, tell me how they can be corrected.'

'Just by self-realisation,' Subham responded.

'Yeah, I realise it was wrong. I should have first tried to understand you, and then I should have politely and gently told you that I am not interested in you by taking you to some alone place. It would have been a much better way. I realise that now. So now can you forgive me?'

'Oh, I was never annoyed with you. It's your life. You don't like to be with me, that's fine, it's your choice. I had one thing for you, though. Hopefully you don't take it the wrong way. I had purchased a Valentine's Day card for you.

But after knowing that I didn't match your class, I tore it into pieces. My tears were out of my control. But when I understood the fact that you can't get everything you want in your life, and I should respect you, I collected each torn up piece of that card and glued them back together. I want to hand over that to you if you don't mind. It's all in the past and I want to get out of it.'

'Please hand it over to me,' Sandhya said.

Subham took it out. Anyone with just one look at the card could tell how much time and effort it must have taken to realign hundreds of pieces together.

Sandhya took it in her hand. 'I am really very sorry, I was actually very rude to you at the time.'

'Do you know, it took five hours to put back the pieces together.'

'What are these spots on the card?'

'My tears,' Subham replied. 'They also got glued into it.'

'I want you to tear this card apart and let it flow into the depths of the sea, where it can rest in peace. I just don't want to look at that anymore. I don't want myself lost in the past any more. I just want to move on from all these. So will you do that for me?'

Sandhya didn't reply.

'And if possible,' Subham continued, 'don't show it to anyone as they will just get a reason to laugh at me again. They don't understand emotions. And yes. It was in the past so let it stay there. You move on towards your goal and let me move on in my direction. I am very thankful to you for sorting out everything with me.'

The best thing for me was that the situation didn't blow me away but I actually took control over it and logically handled it. Yes, there was a time when I liked you. Now my weight will reduce by at least by 5 kg as I transferred the weight of my emotions onto you.'

'Why did you bring this with your?' asked Sandhya, pointing at the card.

'I had originally planned to purchase a bottle with cork screw. In an evening, after finishing the contents of that bottle, I planned to put that card inside it, lock it with the cork screw, and finally throw it away from me.'

'It would float on the sea for years. If someone got hold of it, they could think about me, think about *why I loved*. But I got a much better option and so handed it over to you, for whom it was once purchased and decorated with lots of love. I had spent a whole night just looking at this. But someone rudely crushed it. Look at destiny now. You, this card and I are altogether, but without any emotional affections for which the whole thing started.'

She wanted to leave her seat but Subham told her, 'What you are doing is not the solution. Sit by my side. Why do you want to escape? This is nothing regarding you. I liked you at that time. You denied, and that's alright. If I didn't like things, I will say no.'

He took the card from her hand. 'Let the card stay with me. I can take better care of it as it was me who lived through it at that point of time. You wouldn't understand as it requires an emotional attachment with it which you don't have. So let me do what I had originally planned. You can go wherever you want now. I just had to take this card from you, For you, this is just a piece of paper but for me, it represents what my life was For last one year.

'You are actually very rude,' Sandhya told Subham, but this time her voice was a little different as if she wants to cry.

'Sometimes it is required for me to be like that. You are getting emotional now. Forget everything I told you as if it's a fairy tale and live your life like you planned to before,' Subham said. 'I just want to clarify that, in that story, at no point of time were you wrong. It's me and my emotions alone which misinterpreted things. So please calm down and try to get some sleep as three hours are still left before we reach Goa.'

Sandhya covered herself with a blanket and fell asleep within 15 minutes.

The bus stopped for evening tea and snacks. Subham gently tried to get up from his seat but something appeared to be entangled with the seat. He looked back. Sandhya was holding onto the corner of his shirt firmly, almost as if she didn't want Subham to go anywhere. He gently loosened her grip on his shirt.

Her blanket slid down. He gently put the blanket over her and tried to come out but again something appeared to be entangled. This time she held Subham's forearm while still deep in sleep. Somehow he managed to loosen her grip and came out of the bus.

He had some evening snacks with some tea. Only a few of his batchmates came out of the bus as most of them where sleeping.

The professor asked Subham about the trip. 'How is the trip going?'

'Good, sir,' he replied.

'Now be quick as two hours of the journey is still left.'

Just then, Arpita came out of the bus. The professor urged her to be quick.

'Okay, sir,' she said and moved towards Subham. 'So how's it going?'

'How's what going? Oh, with Sandhya? Yeah, good,' Subham said. 'She is sleeping right now.'

‘Why does your wrist appear to bruised?’

‘Sandhya held onto it tight in her sleep.’

‘Oh, good. Just be careful. If she had gripped your neck in her sleep, you will have to leave this world.’

‘I don’t need to worry.’

‘Why?’

‘Because I know you will save me.’

‘Do you love someone again?’ Arpita asked him.

‘I don’t repeat mistakes, madam. My whole batch, except for you, dropped me for a girl. It appears that I am the odd one out among all of you. But very soon I will make all of you much more comfortable.’

‘How?’

‘You will know that very soon.’

Just then the professor asked them if they were done. They said yes and soon got back inside the bus.

Subham gently moved to his seat without disturbing Sandhya.

‘Why didn’t you wake me up? I am hungry.’ She was awake.

‘I thought it would not do any good to disturb you from your deep sleep.’

'And yet you disturbed Arpita and allowed her to have breakfast.'

'Why are you feeling jealous of her? She is a real and genuine girl. She herself came out of the bus for some evening snacks.'

'You can't even listen to a word spoken against her.'

'Madam, I actually can't listen to anything wrong regarding *anyone*. It's their life. Let them live it the way they want to.'

'Okay, I agree. Please don't get annoyed with me. I know I am not good enough, but I am trying to be.'

'Who said you are not good? You are actually very good, so continue being yourself. Don't try to change yourself for anyone.' Subham give her some tissue papers and asked her to wipe her face and said, 'from today onwards, I don't want to see any tear tracks on your face.'

Sandhya didn't know what to say to that and just remained static in her seat. Subham took the tissues from her hand and gently wiped her tears from her face. 'Done. Do you want to have some snacks now?'

'Yeah,' Sandhya said, 'but we already left the shop behind.'

'I already bought some snacks for you from the shop when the bus stopped. Now have it.'

She smiled. 'Do you want to have something from this?'

'No. I have already eaten. Stop looking at me and have your snacks.'

'What can I do? These eyes aren't obeying my commands.'

'Now you are just flirting with me.'

'You may interpret it however you like it.' Then added, 'You should say thank you to me for those glasses.'

'Yeah, of course, but why?'

'These glasses add to your smartness and makes you look more intellectual.'

'Oh, really?'

'Yes, it's true. Can I ask you a question?'

'Oh, no, not again,' Subham groaned.

'Only one! Why did you bring snacks for me?'

'Because I thought that at least while having your snacks, you may stay quiet. But seems like I was wrong.'

'You know what?'

'Yes, please tell.'

'You are actually quiet rude.' She turned around to the other side and started talking to individuals of the trip monitoring committee. Her plan was to ignore Subham so that he feels jealous. However, after 15 minutes, when she turned towards him, she found him in fast asleep. This annoyed her.

The sun was about to set. Visibility inside the bus was low now. Sandhya softly moved her hands over his hair and said, 'I am sorry,' with tears in her eyes. She let him sleep.

She looked at him for a long time. She may not get another chance to be this close to him again.

Sudden noises around him woke Subham up. He saw that they had reached their hotel in Goa. Everyone was cheering each other, but Sandhya was quite.

'What happened?' Subham asked. 'Are you not happy to be here? Or are you worried about the fact that you may not get another chance to ask Questions?

Just then, a committee member asked them to sit quietly and handed over a slip of paper to each of them in which there was a room number with their room partner mentioned. Sandhya opened hers. 'I am with Arpita.'

'Subham, who is your room partner?'

'I haven't unfolded it yet. Can you guess who my room partner is?'

'No, I can't.'

'Can you guess?'

'Yes.'

'Who?'

'Probably no one.'

'That's not possible.'

'Okay, I am opening it now.'

Sandhya was surprised. Subham's prediction was right.

'Move on. These things don't affect me much now. And I really do enjoy being alone.'

Sandhya didn't move.

'What?' Subham asked.

She didn't say anything.

'Go, enjoy every second of your life. Take care of yourself... Forget everything I told you like it's a fairy tale.'

'Why; will you not talk to me anymore?' Sandhya demanded.

'Look at your friends. They appear to be so angry with me.'

'Why not? Talking to you is a pleasure for me but I don't know whether I will get the opportunity again or not.'

'I don't care about anyone. You can call me whenever you want.'

'Okay, done.'

'Now please move.'

She moved towards her group, which also includes Arpita, but looked at Subham midway. He was going out of the main gate.

'Hey, hello!' she called out loudly. 'Where are you going?' He probably didn't hear her.

9.

It's Not So Easy To Get Over Emotions

Subham went to the sea shore and sat quietly for some time. Then he went to a bar and purchased a bottle of champagne. To execute his plan but he realised it was really costly so he should not waste its content...so he decided to have it at seashore.

He reached at seashore, looked around to check that no one is seeing him and unscrew the champagne bottle...

With great courage he started to drink but it's taste doesn't suit him but to justify the price of it he continued drinking it with all the events of last 12 months broadcasting in his mind

Suddenly he felt someone's hand on his shoulder

He was frightened to be caught with alcohol and gradually turned to look...

It was his Professor

He was shocked...

But Professor told relax,

'Things like champagne are a total waste of money. They contain only a small amount of alcohol,' the professor told him. 'So don't waste your money.'

Subham tried to apologise and told him

'Sir, I actually just want this bottle. I don't need its contents. But as it was costly so I was emptying its content...'

'What? What will you do with that?'

Subham didn't replied.

'Ohh! It's secret...let it be.'

'Professor also appears to be under some sort of influence of intoxication '

'Subham, have you had any before?'

'No, sir.'

Then stay away from all these after settling down on the beach, the professor asked the bar boy to bring drinks for him.

'Look,' the professor advised, 'it is highly addictive. You can have it occasionally, but don't fall into its trap. Lots of families get destroyed because of it. Secondly, know you limit. This means the amount of alcohol which keeps you comfortable. And the most important thing is, always drink with people with whom you can share things as it removes your inhibitions and a lot of things which shouldn't be out in public come out.'

Professor drink came, 'Do you want to have it?' he asked Subham.

'No, sir. After emptying the bottle of champagne, I understand how it work and as per my feel I reached the limit, I just want to leave, as I have some pending work to do.'

'Ok, I will come with you.'

'No sir! I will do it.'

'Look I can't leave you alone, I reached here following you...so don't try to move anywhere without my permission...'

'Is it clear?'

'Yes sir!'

Professor asked, 'Have you ever thought why I keep my eyes on you.'

'No sir.'

'Actually, I was just like you when I was at the same stage of life as you. I saw myself in you and somehow tried to search my old days in you.'

He smiled.

'How are you feeling now?'

'Good. Actually, sir, all the body ache due to the journey is gone now. There is a feeling of lightness.'

'Now tell me about your champagne bottle.'

'Sir it's just casual...nothing important.'

'Actually sir....'

'Yes carry on... believe me I will not respond to that and keep it as secret...'

'Sir, I had a memory which I got into this medical college. I want to leave it behind me forever. But it is precious for me so I want to keep it alive somewhere in the universe. So today I will put my past inside this bottle and, after applying cork screw, I will let it flow away in this infinite ocean.'

'Tell me her name.'

'l won't, sir. You taught me to take care that I don't say out my secrets in public. And I can't disobey you.'

'You are right. Professor laughed

Okay, now just celebrate this achievement of yours as it's not easy to do so.'

Somehow Subham stood and turned around to keep things away from Professor Eyes...

Took out the card....

Looked at it...

Tried to control his emotions but his tears disobeyed his instructions and started flowing

He was trying his best to hide all these from his Professor...

But Professor sensed it and asked, what happened...don't behave like a child, be a man, complete your job...

He didn't replied, 'He was lost in viewing even the finest details of the card...'

'Do it.'

'Yes sir...'

He now tried to tear the card but didn't tear it...placed the intact card inside the bottle, applied the cork screw tightly.

But instead of throwing it, he was holding it close to his heart.

'What happened now?'

'Nothing sir...can you throw this one into the sea.'

'No...do you job on your own.'

'Move.'

Subham ran and threw the bottle with his full effort so that it land long way from the seashore into the deep sea....

Smile and tears both combined together in his face...

Smile for a win and tears for the loss...

Professor kept his hands on his shoulder.

Good job...

Now come we have to reach hotel for dinner, he gave him bottle of water and asked to wash his face and provided him handkerchief...

He mopped his face

Professor asked...feeling good

He smiled and said yes sir...

As they turned around, they found Sandhya and Arpita.

'What are you people doing here?' the professor asked them.

'Just watching the sea, sir.'

'You probably were not watching anything else, and even if were, there is no need to tell anything to anyone. Take it as a strict instruction,' the professor told them sternly.

Arpita came close to Subham. 'Where were you for so long?'

'I was with Professor.'

'What happened to him? We were really worried about you so we came out in search of you.'

'Leave him, Arpita. He doesn't care about anyone,' Sandhya said.

'Oh, Sandhya, please calm down. I thought I will be back within half an hour,' Subham said. 'But the professor saw me and asked me to go with him. I don't even know how many hours it has been.'

'It's going to be nine now. We have to catch the bus as the group has to go for dinner.'

Now the main problem was the unavailability of taxis. It was a real problem. Subham stopped a taxi, but the driver said the taxi can only accommodate three more individuals as one seat was already occupied.

'Okay,' he said. He called the professor and made him sit at the front. He asked Arpita and Sandhya to sit at the back. Then he closed the door and asked the taxi driver to move.

'How will you come?' Sandhya shouted.

'This taxi can accommodate only three individuals. Don't worry about me. I will figure something out. You are going to be late, just catch the bus.'

Sandhya looked back at him through the glass of the window. Subham smiled at her and waved his hand.

They reached the hotel on time. The bus was about to start. They got into the bus.

Both Sandhya and Arpita took separate window seats. They probably didn't want to share their emotions with each other. Both their eyes were wet.

Finally, they reached the *dhaba* where their dinner was scheduled.

'Sandhya and Arpita, please sit together. And don't leave the hotel without prior information. Do you have any information about Subham?'

They said, 'No.'

Dinner was served but they didn't start. When asked, Sandhya just said, 'I can't have anything' and left the seat. Arpita somehow tried to manage things.

'What's the matter?' they asked.

'She is probably missing her mom and dad,' Arpita said.

'Kindly make her understand. It's only a two-day trip.'

'Okay, I will try.' Arpita also left her seat and went to Sandhya.

'What happened?' she asked Sandhya.

'Nothing' she said.

'Missing Subham?'

'No.'

'Then please have your meal. The whole batch is looking at you. Why don't you have your meal?'

'Because I can't. I can't eat anything until Subham has something too,' Sandhya said.

'Look at this situation now. When he loved, you denied him. When I asked him, "Do you love someone again?", he replied that he didn't repeat his mistakes. You have to accept the fact that whether you like him or not, you *do* miss him.'

'Yes.' Sandhya said, 'it's true. I want to cry but the people around me don't even allow me to do that.'

'Hey, look. Sandhya.'

'What?'

They saw Subham having dinner at their table. They both smiled and went to their table.

Subham smiled. 'Were you waiting for me? Now please start.'

Just then, the boys from the organising team came to him and asked, 'Where did you go without prior information?'

The professor intervened, 'I sent him. Do you have a problem?'

'No, sir.'

'Let him have his dinner then.'

They left.

'Please start with your dinner. I know you people are really annoyed with me, but don't take it out on the food. After dinner, you can tell me whatever you want.'

They finally started on their dinner.

'How did you come?' Sandhya asked.

'Caught a truck, and they dropped me here.'

'How was the truck driver ready to drop you here?'

'I told him that my girl would not take her meal without having a look at me. He said, 'Don't lie, today isn't *karvachauth*.' I said, 'Actually, each day is *karvachauth* for my girl, she may miss looking at the moon but not me. So please help me. With that, I managed to make my way here. So, have you looked at the moon?'

Both Arpita and Sandhya looked at each other and smiled.

'Keep smiling. You look beautiful.'

'Who, Arpita or me?'

'It's better if you people decide that. Now finish it eating. If I talked throughout, you won't be able to have anything.'

'Why?'

'Because you can't avoid listening to every single word I say.'

'Ohh...you totally misunderstood,' Sandhya responded

Subham smiled and said 'Yes, I always misunderstood things...will take care of that.'

'Now please start.'

Now everyone was taking their dinner.

'I am done. Please allow me to leave.' He went to the professor and served him water, vegetables, and *chappatis*. 'Do you want anything else?'

'No. my boy, nothing.'

A voice came from behind Subham. 'Can you serve us too?'

'Sure, why not? Just tell me what you want.'

He helped the *dhaba* boy as it was difficult to serve the whole batch alone.

Finally dinner was over.

10.

Now A Song To Be Sung

On the bus, two seats were vacant. One was close to Arpita and the other was close to Sandhya. He looked at the both of them. The professor asked Subham to ask the bus driver to play some music so that everyone can enjoy the drive back. 'And yes, if possible Ghazal of Jagjit singh should be played,' the professor said. Subham guessed the whiskey in him is now playing its role. He asked the conductor of the bus to obey the instructions but he was told that the music player wasn't in working condition. 'We will get it repaired soon,' he was told.

He informed the professor about the same. 'Okay, no problem,' the professor said. 'No problem'

'You sing ...'

'Sir, I am trying to repair the music system,' Subham replied.

The whole bus laughed, including the professor. 'No,' the professor said. 'I want you to sing.'

'Sir, I had never done this before. Please let me go,' Subham pleaded.

'Everyone has to start at some point of time! It's your turn to start today. I assure you, no one in this bus will react to your voice, so don't think about them! Subham, now you are disobeying me.'

'No no, sir, just give me a minute. I don't dare disobey you.'

'And yes, a Ghazal only.'

Subham asked for a phone from the batchmate sitting nearby.

'Now why do you want a phone? Do you need to Google for singing too?'

'No, sir. I want to search for a ghazal of MR Jagjit singh.'

'You have five seconds left.' The professor asked everyone to keep quiet until his next instruction

'Sir...got a song, whose some lines are known to me, but it's not ghazal.'

'Ohh...sing anything except national anthem.'

The whole bus laughed.

Silence...

So Subham continued.

Jab koi baat bigar jaye, jab koi muskil par jaye

Tum dena saath mera, oo humnawaj

Everyone was just stunned with his voice...

And lost in the song...

After finishing first paragraph he stopped...

Said 'Thank you.'

Demand came to complete the song and provided him lyrics on google...

He smiled and continued

But asked all of them to sing first two lines together...

Whole bus sang together jab koi baat bigar jaye..

With lots of energy

Both Sandhya and Arpita where involved with smile on their face

Everyone appeared to be lost.

Sandhya closed her eyes and just tried to feel.

Once he finished, there were a lot of claps and whistles. The professor appreciated him. Sandhya came to sit by Arpita's side and left her seat for Subham.

Subham just sat at window seat, leaned against the glass of the window and closed his eyes. Suddenly, he smiled.

Looking at him smile, both Arpita and Sandhya smiled instantly.

There was a flow of energy in every individual. The whole bus started singing the same song.

He looked at Sandhya and Arpita. Both of them were also enjoying.

He wanted to stop time at that moment.

Too soon, they reached the hotel. No one wanted to come out of the bus.

'What happened?' the professor asked. 'Please come. Subham will sing again tomorrow!'

Everyone clapped and started coming out of the bus.

As Subham stepped out to come out of his seat, he found Sandhya was about to pass by him so he stopped.

Sandhya also stopped.

Subham gestured at her to move ahead with his hand but she didn't move and just continued to look at him.

'What?' he asked.

'You are really good,' she answered.

'Oh, thank you.'

'I wanted to talk to you,' Sandhya said.

'About singing?'

'Of course not. About you.'

'Okay, I will give you that opportunity.'

'Oh ho! I shall wait for it then,' Sandhya told him.

Arpita, who was waiting outside the bus as the key for their room was with Sandhya, called out to Sandhya, asking her to come.

'Yeah, in a moment!' Sandhya called back.

Subham called Arpita just then. She turned, surprised, and asked sweetly, 'What?'

He handed over something to her and moved towards her. 'Take care of your belongings. I won't always be with you.'

Arpita looked at the thing Subham had handed her. It was her hair clutcher. She wanted to thank him but he had already entered the lift. She ran after him and pressed the button to open the doors of the lift.

She entered the lift. The professor also entered behind her and asked them to wait for Sandhya. Sandhya entered. By now, the display above the door of the lift showed the symbol of the lift being overweight as the professor alone weighed around 100 kg.

Subham got out of the lift and asked them to go ahead. Arpita and Sandhya also came out and said that they will take the stairs instead.

'Yeah, sir, these girls need to lose some weight,' Subham said.

The professor laughed loudly and closed the doors to the lift.

'Why are you looking at me like that?' Sandhya asked.

'Now please don't tell me that you will give me an opportunity to have a look at you.'

All three of them laughed.

After reaching on 2nd floor, Subham told, 'So can I leave now? This is probably your room anyway.'

'On reaching his room, he found it to be already open and found the professor inside.'

'Come, Subham. Take these keys and go to my room. It's in another block and faces the sea. I think I should be here with the rest of the students to look after them.'

Subham was a bit surprised.

'Hey, don't tell me that you are afraid of being alone,' the professor said.

'No. No, sir. I will go there. Good night, sir.' He moved out...

Sandhya was in corridor and looked at tense face of Subham asked, 'what happened?

He explained.

She said, 'that's not fair enough.'

'Tell me do you really afraid to stay alone.'

He responded, 'yes'

'But don't have an option, so I have to go.'

'Bye.'

Sandhya was tensed and was thinking why he has to suffer all the time the other block and entered the room. It was a big room with all kinds of facilitics and a balcony that faces the sea.

He took bath, changed his clothes, and moved to the balcony. It was beautiful.

It was around 11 pm but none of his batch mates were asleep. The girls were enjoying in their own groups and the boys were in their own groups. In the park of hotel... Subham looked at them and got sense of relief that he is not alone, everyone is near by.

So he sat on the balcony chair and watched the waves of the huge ocean.

Suddenly, he heard someone calling his name. He turned around and saw Sandhya standing at her window facing his balcony.

'What?'

'What?' she replied.

He laughed, 'why you are chasing me...'

'That's just a coincidence.'

'I know!'

But now I am relaxed...

'As you are close to me'...laughed again

'How did you get a VIP room?' Sandhya asked him.

'I don't know how but the hotel management offered me this. They probably mistook me for a VIP,' he replied.

'Oh ho, a VIP! What a coincidence, though! My window faces yours!' she said.

'You seem happy about that,' Subham pointed out.

'Yeah, of course. I wanted to talk to you. God heard me and gave me the opportunity.'

'Yeah, right. Now ask away whatever you wanted to ask.'

'Did you complete your job?' Sandhya asked.

'Which job?'

'Did you make your memories immortal today?'

'Yeah. I did. You were watching everything.'

'Yeah. From a distance, though. I couldn't see clearly but I did see you throwing something.'

'Someone is knocking on your door,' Subham pointed out. 'It might be Arpita.'

'Let her knock for some time,' Sandhya replied. 'I want to tell you that it doesn't bother me if someone teases me with your name. I actually feel proud to be the choice of such a brave boy. I know I lost you but it's not your loss, it's mine.'

The knocking on the door grew more and more aggravated.

'She will not let us talk.'

'Ok..good night,' Subham said.

The breeze was felt amazing so he brought a bed sheet with a pillow and a blanket to the balcony. He lied down on the floor of the balcony and fell asleep there.

Sandhya woke up early and looked at the clock. It was 5 am. She turned to look at Arpita. She was fast asleep.

She quietly came close to the window and opened it halfway. She saw Subham in fast asleep in the balcony.

She continued to look at him. Arpita came behind her.

'What are you doing?'

Sandhya tried to close the window but Arpita had already reached the window.

'Oh my God. Couldn't have a morning better than this! Look, Sandhya! Look at how innocent he looks while sleeping! But what is he doing here?'

'I don't know,' said Sandhya and closed the window.

'Hey, why did you close it?'

'I just opened it to have a look at the view outside. I am done.'

'Oh really?'

'Okay, come on. It's 6 am already and, as per schedule, we have to leave at 8 am.'

'Okay, then, get yourself ready first.'

'Hey, Subham! Please wake up, we are getting late,' she called out but he didn't respond.

About 15 minutes later, Sandhya came back. 'I am done,' she told Arpita.

'I can't believe the girl who takes at least an hour to get ready came back so fast. Please take your time. I am not in any hurry.'

'I don't want to put any makeup.'

'Why?'

'Who looked at me for so long? Not even don't want to have by my side. I don't want to adorn myself for anyone else.'

'Okay, as you wish,' Arpita said. 'But please make sure Subham wakes up otherwise he will miss the bus.'

Sandhya didn't respond.

Arpita got ready. At 7:30 am, Subham was still sleeping.

'I think we should leave,' Arpita said.

Both of them reached the bus. The professor came soon. Sandhya somehow gathered the courage to tell him that Subham still hasn't turned up.

'There is still 15 minutes left. He will come,' he reassured her.

'No, sir. He is still sleeping.'

'Oh, how did you know that?'

Arpita took over the conversation at this point. 'When we opened our window, we found him sleeping in his balcony.'

'Come with me, show me the way to his room.'

They reached Subham's room and pushed the call bell button several times.

At last, the professor called his name loudly.

'Yes, sir, came his reply. Within seconds, he had opened his door and looked at all of them.

'Good morning,' he said gently.

'You have only ten minutes in your hands. I want you inside the bus by the end of it,' the professor said.

'Okay, sir,' Subham said and closed the door.

All of them smiled and moved on.

11.

The Real Tease

Subham reached the bus on time and entered the bus before anyone else. The professor looked at his watch. 'Subham, you are right on time. It will take ten more minutes for the bus to start though. Why did you occupy your seat so early?'

'Actually, sir, I don't want to sit at the back so I occupied my seat right away,' he replied.

Arpita, who just entered the bus, said, 'He is right, sir.' She sat on the seat next to Subham.as she enjoys teasing Sandhya...

Sandhya looked at Arpita and sat on the window seat just behind Subham.

Subham just looked to his side and then at the back. 'Hey. How are you?'

'Who are you asking?'

'Both of you,' Subham answered.

'Fine. Thank you,' Sandhya replied. She looking at Arpita and smiled.

'Did the both of you really make so many enemies for me?'

'What?'

'Just look around. All the boys are looking at me. They probably want to meet up with me alone and teach me a lesson.'

'I don't care,' Arpita said. 'Anyway, that's your problem. And I know no one would even dare involve themselves with you.'

'How can you say that so confidently?'

'It's simple. Because I am with you.'

'Oh thanks a lot. *Now* I feel secured.'

'And I am not like you, I will always be with you,' Arpita said.

'Thank you. I am pleased to hear these words. Sandhya, do you want to say something?'

'Does everything needs to be said? Some words should be felt without hearing them,' Sandhya replied.

'Yeah, you are right, but you also need the kind of an individual who can do that. By the way, you still look good without make up.'

'Can I ask you something?' Arpita asked.

'Yeah, sure.'

'What kind of food do you like?'

'Why?' Subham asked.

'I have to learn as I don't know how to cook.'

'I am strict non-vegetarian,' Subham told her, 'and don't worry, I know how to cook.'

'Me too,' Arpita replied.

'But I am a strict vegetarian,' Sandhya said.

There was a few seconds of silence after that.

Leaning against the glass of the window, Subham asked Sandhya, 'Have you ever thought about why we both are so different from each other? We don't have a single common ground between us.'

Sandhya replied after a few seconds, 'If you ask me, I will become non-vegetarian.'

'Hey, don't change yourself for anyone.'

'I want to match with you at least in one habit.'

'There's no need for that,' Subham said. 'I can cook vegetarian food too. Why would you want to sacrifice anything to become a hero in someone else's heart?' Subham responded

'It's not sacrifice,'

'It's being understanding.'

'You shouldn't change yourself just to be liked by someone because that won't last for long. But if you respect and understand others' emotions, it will last forever.'

Then why you fail to establish understanding whom you liked...

Subham looked at Arpita. With red eyes, she blinked her eyes and smiled 'Your failure is actually the first step towards your understanding. Making mistakes isn't a crime, but not learning from them is. I know the exact reasons but it doesn't matter to anyone anymore. Is there any more personal questions you want to ask me, Arpita?'

'No, but you people have to pay the price for all these lectures?'

Sandhya gave her purse to him and asked him to continue.

'So I am opening this purse to take my consultancy fee.' He opened the purse and got the comb out. He held it out. 'Comb your hair properly.' he asked Sandhya.

'Why?'

'Madam, this is a part of my consultancy fee. And keep the rest of the things with you as I don't need them right now.'

'Subham, you didn't brought anything with you.'

'What things?'

'Oh ho! Will you not go into the sea? You will need another set of clothes to change into after.'

'Do you both have clothes with you?'

Both of them said, 'yes.'

'Good. Have a good time there. I actually have some different plans.'

'What is it?'

'Nothing special. I will be returning with you though,' he said.

'Why don't you just say that you are scared of the sea? Sandhya asked.

'Yes, you are right. And also, I don't know how to swim.'

'Don't worry, I know that.'

'I have an extra set of t-shirt and trousers, you can have that,' Arpita said.

'Live without me,' Subham replied.

'Why are you being like this? We don't need you to keep ourselves alive,' Sandhya said.

'I know that, I was just wanted to hear it from you.'

By then the bus had reached the area near the beach. All the students came out of the bus with joy and started going towards the sea.

Subham was the last to come out of the bus. He went to a place where there was no one and lied down on the sand. He wanted to go with his batch mates into sea, but he knew that no one likes him, especially now that Sandhya or Arpita talks to him. He also wanted to create some distance from the both of them., so he felt that it was better for everyone if he stays alone and let others enjoy.

12.

Now It's All About Survival

Just then the professor came up 'My boy, what are you doing

Just watching them enjoying.'

'Why don't you joined them?'

'Actually I didn't bring clothes with me...'

'Ok...'

'Anyway I want to tell you one thing...'

'I understand everything. The place that you made your second home was visible from my second floor room and I saw you every day. Sometimes I went out to look after you when you slept there and sat on the bench nearby. Not because I wanted that but because my wife looked after you every moment you were there. I don't know whether you are aware or not but we have everything we wanted in our lives except the honour of being a father and a mother. So seeing you in such a situation, my wife's maternal instincts came into play and I had to took care of you. The peak of this emotional attachment was that my wife kept checking in between by the help of a lightning torch whether I was taking care of you. I didn't want to tell you these things but emotions are really selfish. Today they made me to speak out about everything without caring about what you think about it.'

'Sir,' Subham began, 'this is an honour for me, and I promise you whenever anyone talks about me along with my father and mother, you and madam will get the same honour as my own parents.'

'Thank you. I probably took more than a little whiskey to gather the courage to tell you everything,' the professor confessed.

'Leave the whiskey behind. If you really like me, I don't want my loved one to be intoxicated they say that they love me.'

The professor threw the full bottle of whiskey away. 'Are you happy now?'

'Yeah,' Subham said. 'Buy me at least five sets of shirts and pants.'

'Okay, I will. Come with me.'

Subham stood up and hugged him. 'I was just joking. I don't need anything. I am blessed enough to receive this amount of love and affection.'

The professor turned his face the other side.

'What happened?' Subham asked.

'Nothing,' the professor replied.

Subham gave him his handkerchief and asked him, 'You ask those tears not to dare come out of your eyes.

The rest, I will take care of.'

The weather was very pleasant. The breeze was refreshing but all of a sudden, panicked voices could be heard from the side his batch mates where enjoying in.

Subham could see a baby struggling with the waves of the sea., nearby shore He ran towards the sea shouted for lifeguards., but when he didn't find anyone to help, he jumped in with a tube he found nearby and tried to reach to the child as he didn't appeared much distant from shore

Sandhya, knowing he didn't know how to swim well, started crying. Arpita tried to go after him into the sea to save him, but by then, the lifeguards were in action and had already stopped everyone.

They began the search but even after half an hour of searching, couldn't find anyone. The siren could be heard to warn against the high tides accompanied by heavy rain.

The professor stopped his crying and asked everyone to go inside the bus but all of his students denied. They all stood at a safe distance from the sea shore but didn't move inside the bus. The mother of that baby was in severe panic.

Sandhya asked Arpita to bring him back anyhow. 'I have to confess a lot of things to him,' she said. Both of them were in tears.

'He has to come back anyhow,' Arpita said, 'he wouldn't dare leave us alone.'

Their tears continued to flow.

The professor was in shock, almost as if he lost his own son. After a lot of attempts, the rescue team returned without the victims as the tides were really high.

'We are arranging for helicopters for the search,' they told the professor and ask everyone to back to hotel

The professor strictly instructed all the students to get into the bus. They entered the bus with wet eyes. The professor asked the driver to drop them at the hotel.

'And you, sir?' the driver asked.

'Please forgive me but I can't be back with you. My student is fighting for his life. I will wait for him till I find him. As I can't leave him in between the fight, otherwise he will complain to me that even I left him.'

All the students came out of the bus. The professor stopped trying to control his emotions and broke down into tears. The siren beeped loudly and the sirens of the ambulances began to ring.

Something had happened.

They all went to the sea shore and saw someone carrying a child and coming towards them. With a life guard, security personnel didn't allow students to move and stopped them

They were still far away and it was difficult to recognise whether the two were actually the ones for whom they were waiting for but as they came closer, the mother of the baby broke the security barriers and ran towards them.

Subham handed over the child to her. The mother tried to touch Subham's feet but he held her and stopped her.

Subham was not feeling good and felt a bit disoriented, like he was suffering from vertigo. He tried to hide it and moved towards ambulance but just after a few steps, he fell down and lost consciousness.

The medical team rushed towards him from the other side. Only the professor was allowed to look at him.

He was shifted inside the ambulance and was given oxygen. The ambulance siren started beeping loudly and it took off at full speed to reach the nearby hospital.

All the students were sent to their rooms in their respective hotels. Lunch was served but Arpita and Sandhya didn't eat. Neither have uttered a single word since the incident.

Upon reaching their room, Arpita moved to window and opened it. She found someone there.

'Subham!' she shouted.

Sandhya ran to the window.

Subham moved closer to their side of the balcony.

'What?'

'How are you?'

'Good. You actually made us so nervous. I have never felt tremors because of nervousness like that before. After seeing you unconscious, I just wanted to hold you but security didn't allow me to go near you.'

'Will you drink whiskey with me tonight?'

'What?'

'Nothing. Where is Sandhya?'

'She went to the temple as soon as she saw you. She had vowed something for your life. You have turned an atheist into a believer.'

'I destroyed everyone's trip,' said Subham.

'Hey, please don't say that. Actually, you are our hero.'

The call bell of Subham's room rang. 'Stay right there,' he told Arpita and went to open the door.

He was surprised to find Sandhya there.

'How are you?' she asked.

'Okay now,' he replied.

She applied a *tika* on his forehead and gave him some *prasad.*

'What occasion is this for?' he asked her.

'For your well-being,' she replied. 'I will talk to you later.'

'Hey, Sandhya. I think you lost your slippers.'

'No,' Sandhya said, 'I left them in my room as I had to go to the temple barefoot.'

When he returned to the balcony, Arpita smiled and asked if it was Sandhya.

Sandhya appeared at the window at that. Subham asked them to get ready for their evening trip.

'It's almost time. The bus will start soon,' he told them.

'Are you coming?'

'No. I have been advised to take a day's rest. You guys go and enjoy.'

The bus departed from the hotel.

He ordered room service to bring tea and some snacks

He took his bed sheet and pillow to the balcony and looked at the sunset with waves of the sea going up and down. He had to battle for his life through that today. Looking on them, they appeared to be so beautiful to him but now, after his close encounter with them, he knows how lucky he to return alive was.

This episode created a deep impression on his mind. He wanted to come out of it and celebrate his new birth.

But he wanted to do this alone.

All the things were in place, the noise of the waves, the pleasant breeze, delicious food and a proud feeling inside him.

He was just missing someone with whom he can share all these painful experience

Honestly speaking, Sandhya still occupied a corner of his heart, but he can't say this to her and so he always tried to give her the impression that she was his past and nothing more. On the other hand, Arpita helped him come out of his tearful days. She reminded him of his value and told him to be with the one who likes you, cares for you, and if she asked Subham to be with him for the rest of his life, he won't be able to deny that.

He didn't know what to do and when the situation came to be like this.

He didn't know who to be with.

Anyway, he left everything to time as with time, everything changes.

But he wanted someone with him right now, someone who he could talk about a lot of things with. But there was no one there, except for him and his loneliness.

He just sent a prayer to God, thanking God for giving him another chance to live, and went to the mirror to look at the *tilak* Sandhya had applied on his forehead. This was by the same girl who once make him cry.

Why are emotions so strong that they give off the sense that you can't live without someone. Why does the brain not come into play and control all these emotions?

He thought about why he cried so much for Sandhya and why he liked her so much.

Why was a single glimpse of her enough to turn his day beautiful? Why did her smile bring a smile on his face?

He didn't even talk to her or understood her yet he wanted her to be a part of his life.

He didn't have any explanation for all these and felt that it is true that love can't be felt after calculations. It just happens. The how's and why's cannot be explained in 99.99% of the cases.

It's a beautiful emotion when felt from both sides but creates a situation of panic when it is felt only from one side, especially when you hear from that special someone that you do not belong to her class.

Yeah, she is beautiful, smart and intelligent. And he is not. Up to that level but how can he make his emotions understand the fact that one should love or like someone only when one accurately analyses things regarding class and smartness?

He did the mistake and suffered. Even after so much, he had never behaved rudely towards her because if you like someone, you don't try to hurt them. You take care of them whenever you get the chance.

The best thing to do when you know that she or he doesn't like you is to keep your distance from them. One shouldn't try to possess their emotion by any means and should try to move on.

Yeah you liked them, and nobody can stop you from doing that, but should you just want them to be happy, even if it means they are with someone else.

After dealing with a lot of questions and answers inside himself, he asked mirror, 'Am I not good enough?' and smiled.

His mood was good now and his thoughts were clear.

He moved to balcony and sip the cup of tea in the hand.

The call bell rang. He went to door and asked, 'Who is it?'

'The hotel staff, sir.'

He opened the door

'What?'

'Sir, the bill.'

He cleared the bill.

'Sir, do you need anything else?'

'I will call you if I need anything.'

He closed the door and went to the balcony again.

There were clouds in the sky now and the breeze brought in some amount of moisture with them.

Subham just sat on his bed sheet with his pillow beneath his elbow and felt everything.

The call bell rang again. He was annoyed now and called out, 'The door is open. Please come in.'

The doorbell rang again.

'Please come in,' he said.

The doorbell didn't ring after that.

He didn't care enough and continued to be in the same posture

Just then, the call bell rang again. He stood up, went to the door, and pulled it open.

'Hello.' It was Sandhya and Arpita.

'Hello, Subham,' they replied.

'What were you doing? Sandhya asked

'Nothing special.'

'Then why did the colour on your face fade away just by seeing us?' she asked.

'I was not expecting you people,' he replied.

'Can we come inside?'

'You didn't go with the bus?'

'No.'

'Why?'

'We planned to celebrate your birthday.'

'My birthday? It's in November.'

'For us, it's today. We saw you coming out of the sea as if it's a rebirth.'

'Okay, thank you.'

'Throw us party!'

Sandhya said he has already arranged things for his own party.

'Come to the balcony and see the arrangements for yourself,' Subham said.

'Wow, that's great. I think we are disturbing you. You were probably waiting for someone else.'

'Nothing like that. I actually wanted someone with me but was not expecting both of you. Please give me the honour of having guests like you.'

'What do you say, Sandhya? Should we join him or not?' Arpita asked.

'Since he is requesting so much, we should accept it,' Sandhya replied.

'Sorry, ma'am, but only one of you are allowed. I cannot handle two girls at the same time,' Subham said.

They both looked at each other.

'Take it easy. Please come and join me,' Subham said.

Actually all the snacks are non-vegetarian., if you want to have veg snacks kindly order it as I don't have that much of money to pay the bill

,' All of them laughed

Just then, Arpita's phone started ringing.

'My uncle is calling,' she said. 'He lives here in Goa and wants to meet me.'

'First pick up the phone at least.'

'Oh, you are in the hotel? I am coming.' She turned to Sandhya. 'Come, Sandhya.'

'I'll be here. You go and come soon after meeting your uncle

'Please, Arpita. I want to talk to him, please leave me with him for a moment.'

'Okay, as you wish.'

'So, how are you?' Sandhya started.

'Are you asking this to me?' Subham asked.

'Of course. No one else is here with us.'

'I am fine.'

'So why did you jump into the sea when you knew that you can't swim well?'

'I don't know. I just couldn't see an innocent child struggle for his life in front of me.'

'You do realise that you could have lost your life in that?'

'Honestly speaking, I thought I had got the tube which will protect me and as the child was not far away., I will jump and catch him and will come back....but the situation was different as I hold the child, the high tides waves bounce us away from shore and that turned into a nightmare for me., but at that time I found a huge rock by my side...I was thinking only of that child in the middle of the sea. I just accepted that May be I not come out of it. So I lifted him and kept him high on the rock. I was struggling to keep him there as the high tides kept trying to pull me deep inside the sea. There came a point of time when I decided to surrender but the child's eyes kept telling me that once I surrender, nobody will be able to help him. That gave me the ultimate strength and I decided to fight back. Somehow I got myself over that rock and held him firmly.

And waited there for help

'Each min of wait was appearing to be hour long

'I want to salute you,' Arpita said.

'Hey, you didn't go to meet your uncle,' Subham said.

'No. How could I miss your bravery?'

'Hey, it was not bravery. ...

It was just a chance and decision taken by instinct... otherwise I am so scared of sea that I even don't go near it

Subham stood up and moved towards the corner of the room. Sandhya observed the numerous abrasions on Subham's hand and feet.

'Are you taking any medicine?' she asked.

'You are no less than any medicine for me,' he said and laughed

'Arpita, go and meet your uncle. Sandhya, please go with her as it is dark now.'

Unwillingly, Sandhya had to go with her.

Honestly, Subham just wanted to be alone.

After thinking for a few moments, he looked at the chair in front of him.

Sandhya was sitting in front of him.

'Hey...'

'What are you doing here, when you came back...' Subham was actually surprised...

Why didn't you finished the snacks yet...?

Actually I don't want to have it alone

'When did you Came back?'

'Actually I didn't go,' Sandhya replied.

'Why do you not like me here?'

'Why do you take me the wrong way all the time? You wanted to ask me the rest of your thousand questions that you had in your mind, so you didn't go. Am I right?'

'Yes, probably. I just wanted to be with you for some time,' Sandhya told him. And asked him to arrange some veg snacks

'Okay, let me arrange something for you since you are a guest in my party,'

'The restaurant is closed and will only open at dinner.' she said

'I know. Just let me arrange something. Sit comfortably.'

Within a few moments, he was serving Sandhya a plate of hot noodles with tomato sauce. The peculiar thing about it was that he had written 'just for you' with sauce on the noodles.

Sandhya was completely surprised. She looked at Subham. 'How did you do that?'

'This room is equipped with a tea maker. I cooked in that,' he told her. 'And that sauce was with me for my snacks.

Now please start...

She held the plate and clicked a picture of the plate.

'What are you doing?' Subham asked. 'It's was just casually done.'

'I want to capture this piece of creativity,' Sandhya replied.

'Eat it.'

'You can have your snacks too as you are no more alone

Sure.'

'Now ask what you want to know

'How are you?'

'Good. Why?'

'I thought you might have body-aches.'

'Pain. Yes. It is there but don't know how the happiness of survival overshadowed it

Finish your meal otherwise you will tell me that I don't even have the class to honour my guests. Now why are you looking at me like that?'

'I just want one thing from you.'

'Yes?'

'Forgive me,' Sandhya said.

'For what?'

'For hurting your emotions.'

'Oh you really are still a kid. I already told you, that was all my fault. I should ask you to forgive me as you unnecessarily get teased because of me. Just drop all your guilt regarding this right here today itself and enjoy your life. Don't even try to look at me or my name.'

'I promised you I will help you get out of all this. Just give me a few days.'

'What will you do in the upcoming days?'

'If my plan succeeds, I will leave you all,' Subham answered. 'Then when people stop seeing me, they will forget me, and this will make things easier for you.'

'Where are you going?'

'Nowhere. And please don't think that I am going to leave this world. ...what tell me where you are going?'

'Ohh! Just joking!'

Sandhya didn't utter a single word.

'Hey, what happened?'

'I don't know, Subham. I was thinking. How will I live without seeing you if you leave.'

'Hey, what?'

'Please don't leave us.'

'I was just joking, but what happened to you?'

'I don't know. You are in my mind all the time. Wherever I look, I see your face. I want to be with you all the time. I want to hear your voice and nothing else. I want to talk to you all the time. You don't like me anymore, I know that. But what can I do? Tell me. Your thoughts don't leave me for even a single second. Hiding in the washroom, I try to stop my tears, but they continue to flow. Tell me the solution to this. When you smile, I want to smile. When you were lost in the sea, I felt as if I lost you. It will be impossible for me to live. Do you know, I haven't slept for two nights in a row? I just passed my nights seeing you in this balcony, sleeping. I was wrong. Actually *I* didn't belong to *your* class. But by the time I realised that, it was already too late for me to tell you these things. I am extremely sorry. I will not ask you to give me some space in your life but at least allow me to look at you every day. I can't think about the day when I won't see you anymore.'

'Hey, just relax.'

'Yes, please. I understand that hearing all these things must not be pleasant for you.'

'Look, Sandhya. I understand your emotions but it's too early for me to commit as I had already taken some steps that I can't come back from.'

He moved close to her and put his hands on her head and asked her to be relaxed, everything will be alright...don't you worry

After an event full trip all of them returned back to college happily.

Now after 5 days results of their first year MBBS was expected. So, these 5 days were tense for all.

The results of the final examination of the first year MBBS students have been declared. Subham secured the first rank. Everyone congratulated him.

However he was not happy. Sandhya noticed

The very next day....

13.

The Very Next Day

'Welcome, everyone,' the professor said. 'The second year of MBBS. Today is a proud moment for all of us.

Principal Sir, will you tell us about that?'

'It's indeed a proud moment for all of us,' the principal said. 'One of our students have secured the top rank in the Armed Forces Medical Scholarships Examination. They will now sponsor one of our student till his super-specially degrees, Yes, we will miss him as he probably has to leave us and go with them. I don't know the exact procedure. But the boy has requested me not to take his name. He feels that his presence or absence here doesn't matter to us.., don't know why he think like this

Anyway, life moves on and we wish him all the best.'

There was a pin-drop silence in the whole of class.

'Today we came here to wish you all the best for your second year course and to motivate you people to make us proud as your one of the Batch mates did

'Professor, I think we should name him, as he has left for his destination, so our promise will not break...and actually he deserves an applause.'

'Sir...as you wish.'

'Subham Saket is his name, he secured top rank...'

'Today morning he will leave for PUNE.'

'KINDLY GIVE huge round of applause for him.'

'As a principal I am very proud of him.'

The whole class stood and clapped...

Except Sandhya... who appeared to be in shock.

Professor noticed it...

And after class he called Sandhya and Arpita

Told them look we should be happy for him, I know it's painful...but we should search happiness in his happiness...

And he had promised that he will come back after a year approximately

As there is one provision that the top 3 students of their final semester students can move to their choice of college and after completing their study they have to report back to headquarters of armed forces...

Sandhya asked...sir can you do me a favour

What

Kindly give me his Mobile number ...I want to talk to him.

Look till now he had probably entered the campus and there Mobile phones are not allowed

I asked him to call once he get opportunity for that, and I will definitely ask him to talk to you.

Actually he requested for your mobile number, but I didn't have that...

Give me your number ...I will give him once he call

Next day Professor called them and told he is alright but stressed, as it appeared with his voice...

I am really worried about him. Look I gave him your number. He will call in a day or two. As they are allowed to call only thrice a week...

And I want you people to boost his morale. I don't want him to succumb to the stress of the new college and our expectations

Professor left after that...

Now the wait starts for call...

She looked hundred times a day on her mobile for any call or message from Subham.

Always hold phone in her hand...checking for its network connection, battery status, but the call didn't came.

After few days, suddenly a beep appeared on his phone.

She checked a message was there,

She opened it...

A base phone number was there...

Call immediately...tell them that you are from my home and ask them to call me

Subham

Now Sandhya called Arpita and told her the details

Arpita said... 'ok, then call.'

She said what I will tell about my relationship with Subham as they allow family members to call...

Ok. Tell them that you are his sister...after hearing this Sandhya lifted pillow and hit it hard to Arpita and started laughing with Arpita ...

Finally she made a call....

14.

Finally She Made A Call

Yes, it is the medical wing. Who do you want to talk to?''

'Subham Saket.'

'Okay.'

'Can you give me an appointment for talking to him?'

'Kindly give us your details.'

'I am from his home.

Namaskar.'the voice came from other side

'Please hold for a moment. He is right here.'

'Hey, Subham sir! There is a call for you.'

He picked up the phone. 'Hello?'

However, no voice could be heard from the other side.'

'Hello?' he said again.

'*Yaad aa gayi hamari. Humko to laga ki bhul gaye ho tum,*' Sandhya replied.

'I am alright. I am taking my meals on time, which includes talking to you.'

'I never miss that.'

'How are you?'

'Just existing. You took everything of mine with yourself,' Sandhya replied.

'Okay, I will check my luggage and keep all your things carefully.

'Why you talking like this? Is someone there close to you?'

'Yes'

'You seem to be facing a lot of difficulties there,' Arpita said.

'Yes, but this is a part and parcel of life. I am trying my best to live a proper disciplined life,' Subham answered.

'When will you come back?'

Subham didn't reply.

'Hello? Hello? Are you there?'

'Yes, I am trying my best, but I can't say anything. Take care of yourself.'

'Just give your best...don't worry about results...!"

'I will try.'

'What is this beep all about?'

'Our time is about to be over. Keep smiling. Don't get worried about me. We will talk next week.'

'Miss you.'

'I don't as I don't forget things. I carry them with me. Only ten seconds left now. Bye. Over and out.'

The phone got disconnected. There was a complete silence on both sides.

Subham controlled his emotions with a lot of courage and sat down on a nearby bench. Sandhya hid her face with a blanket. Arpita went to her room without uttering a single word.

Subham repeatedly thinking about why he was so emotional. Why was he unable to forget them and live a comfortable disciplined life here during his studies?

He looked at the rest of the boys playing volleyball noisily and cheerfully. He can't enjoy a single minute here as he has to get a good grade in all the parameters, studies, fitness, discipline, sports, etc., so that he can get back to Sandhya

He kept thinking about why he had loved, as it was the beginning of all his emotional distractions but later thought about what a blessing it was that God had sent people who shower such an amount of love on him and motivated me to perform excellently.

His batch mates called out to him. 'Come here quickly! You have to save us! We are five points behind.' Subham ran to them and finished the match within five minutes by defeating the opponents.

'Did you get to drink plenty of energy drinks through that phone call?' they asked him.

'Excellent, Subham,' Coach complimented him.

'Thank you, sir.'

According to their schedule, they had to wake up at 4:30 am, gather on the grounds at 5 am, and run for minimum of 5 km. Breakfast was served was at 7 am and classes started from 8 am and continued until 4 pm. Evening snacks were served at 5 pm. After two hours of sporting activities, dinner was served at 9 pm.

Whenever he felt like giving up, he was reminded of his promise to go back and he started again.

Arpita saw Sandhya after a day at dinner as she had given up on her meal to wait for Subham's phone call.

'How are you?' Arpita asked.

'Better.'

'He is good, actually. Very good.'

'Who?'

'My boyfriend.'

'Who is your boyfriend?'

'You don't know?'

'No.'

'Subham.'

'Hey, Arpita, he is mine,' Sandhya told her.

'You denied him earlier. Do you not remember?' Arpita asked.

'Yes, I did. And it was the biggest mistake of my life. Otherwise he would have been here with me all the time. Hey, Arpita. I don't know whether he likes me or not, but I can't live without him.'

'Why is it so?'

'I don't know.'

'You like him.'

'No. I *love* him. And I don't know whether he will ever be able to understand the depth of that love. But I will wait for him, without tears. Because I am a girlfriend of an army personnel and tears have no place in that life.'

'I know you like him too. Yes or no?'

'Yes, but I will tell you some things later on.'

'What things?'

'He is mine and only mine.'

'Calm down and believe in your love.'

Sandhya phone rang.

'Hey, it's the professor.'

'Sir?'

'I had to ask something.'

'Yes, sir. Please.'

'Do you have Subham's number? My wife tries to call him every day about a hundred times but his phone is switched off every time.'

'Sir, mobile phone are not allowed there. Subham is okay,' Sandhya answered.

'How do you know that? Please give me the number.'

'I am forwarding it to you, sir. It's the medical wing base's phone number. Ask for Subham. They will ask your details. Tell him you are his father, only then will they give you an appointment to talk to him. I don't know the time schedule for these calls and he will mostly reply in yes or no.'

The professor called Sandhya back.

'Sir?'

'This is Madam talking and I just wanted to say thank you for making the phone call with Subham possible. You might not know but since we don't have a child of our own, we treat Subham as our own child. Just one more thing. He is going through a tough phase so while talking to him, avoid being too emotional and become his strength instead. I understand him to the extent that I know everything about him even if he doesn't speak out loud about it. He is some facing problems in adapting to the environment there as the the first year students there are already well adjusted and are enjoying their time there. But he is fighting hard to both adjust as well as to perform. We should not open a third door of problems for him. We should hide our emotions and let him fight his fight. Hopefully you understand, Sandhya.'

'Yes, ma'am.'

'Also, tell Arpita the same thing.'

'Okay.'

'Good night.'

Since the phone was on speaker, Arpita heard everything.

'Is he a magician?' she asked. 'How many hearts is his home in?'

'I don't know, but only a mother can think in this manner. Every word she said was accurate.' Sandhya realised it now and decided to control all her emotions in front of him. She would express everything at once when she meets him.

She constantly looked at the calendar and counted the days; a week would pass by until she got to hear his voice again.

Soon, the day came. She asked Arpita to make the call.

'Why?' Arpita asked.

'Arpita, please. I don't know why but I don't feel good.'

'What? Do you think I am a rock? I don't know what to tell you... I also count days but... Never mind. I will make the call.'

The phone rang.

The same voice answered. 'Yes, the medical wing.'

'Can I talk to Subham?'

There was a few seconds of silence. 'Ma'am, it will not be possible today.'

'Why? I am calling from his home,' Arpita said.

'I am sorry to tell you but Subham sir got injured an hour ago while horse riding. He is hospitalised right now.'

'Hey, what are you saying?!' Is he okay? Give me his contact number right now! I want to talk him right away. I have a right to!'

'Ma'am, please wait. Let me try to connect the phone.'

A voice answered from the other side. '*Jai hind*, sir.'

'There is a call from Subham sir's home and they want to talk him right now.'

'Okay, connect me to them.'

'Hello, ma'am. I am *Kamal* Abhimanyu. Subham is just suffering from a mild injury. We are taking care of him, so please don't worry.'

'Please, I just want to hear his voice. For a few seconds at least,' Arpita pleaded.

'Okay, let me see.'

He connected the call to the ward and asked the nurse to connect Subham on the line.

'Hey, my hero. How are you?'

'Fine, sir,' Subham answered.

'There is a call for you. Talk to them. I will be keeping my handset down so you can talk without any hesitation. Take care. I want you back as soon as possible, okay?'

'Aye, aye, sir.' Then, a moment later, 'Hello?'

'How are you?'

'Hey, Arpita! How are you? I am good, there were just some abrasions and lacerations. Will be alright in a few days.'

'Are you there for studying or horse riding?' Arpita demanded.

'They prepare a soldier first and I am proud of that.'

'Why do you always make us cry?'

'What can I do? You guys can at least cry but I can't even do that. Why don't you guys forget me? I don't know whether I will ever be able to bring a smile on your faces. Just forget me, please. I can't see any more tears in your eyes because of me. It is more painful than my wound. Are you busy in wiping your tears?'

'I don't know. Why don't you forget us?'

'Never forget your loved ones. We are taught that here every day.'

'Hey, Sandhya, I know you guys have me on speaker and you are listening to me. Be brave.'

'I don't want to be brave,' Sandhya said. Give me any other option.'

'Come and live with me.'

'Tell me the place, date, and time. I will come.'

'At least you spoke now.'

'I only give you tears and nothing else, yet you want to be with me.'

'I know. But even a single word from your side makes it all worth it.'

'If I knew that I only had a few seconds left of my life, I would want to spend those moments with you.'

'Is there anything else you wanted to ask?'

'No,' Sandhya said.

'Then you don't have any choice but to be brave. I want my sweet girlfriend to be my strength. Don't tell the professor anything regarding this.'

'How are you speaking so freely today?'

'My *karnal* has given me that freedom today.'

Everything is alright..just take care of yourself ..I am trying hard and will be soon with you people

Ok...take care

Will wait for you...

Days passed with occasional talks between them.,

The irony was that both of them try to hide their own pain and tries to console the other one

Gradually a year passed and Subham appeared for his examination...

Now no phone calls were allowed.

One month passed without communication with Sandhya...

Sandhya had her examination date announced after a month...but her focus was on Subham's examination....but was unable to get the details.

15.

I Always Thought, Will You Ever Realise"

One morning...Sandhya got a call inside her hostel that someone came to meet him...a boy named Subham...

She came running out of the hostel but couldn't find Subham.

She was actually out of breath...thinking may be someone joked with her...

Just then Subham put his hand on her shoulder from behind and asked, 'Who are you searching for?'

Sandhya turned around at that.

It was Subham.

He had changed drastically. His haircut was that of a typical army personnel. He had lost all of his extra fat and now appeared to be really fit. He was well dressed too.

'Hey, why are you looking at me like that?' Subham asked.

'You are looking really handsome,' Sandhya replied after a few seconds of silence.

'But you deteriorated.'

'All because of you,' Sandhya replied.

'Trust me, I am with you and I'm not going to leave this earth.'

'How are you come here so suddenly?' Sandhya asked..,

Actually after the examination leave was declared to go home I thought to meet you and then go to home...

'They reached the park nearby. It was completely silent there.

Subham turned to Sandhya and asked her to sit on the bench. 'How are you, Sandhya?'

'I don't know. If you are fine, just assume that I am fine too.'

'Hey, I am really tired. I want to sleep. It's probably been more than a year now since I last slept properly.' Subham told

She looked into his eyes and touched her hair with her hand.

'I can understand that.'

'Why have you changed so much?' Subham asked

'You look like you haven't combed your hair properly for months!' Subham said.

'I was actually waiting for you. I was waiting for the day when I will adorn myself for you. But you came so suddenly. That I didn't have the time for that.

Actually, all my desires left once you were gone.'

'Hey, I only give you tears. Have you realised that?' Subham asked.

'Each drop of tear I shed for you is an asset for me,' Sandhya said.

'I may not come back to this medical college.'

'Don't worry. I can wait for you my entire life. Five years do not matter much to me. Hey, Subham. I just want to clarify some things today. I like you. I want to be with you all the time, if not physically, at least in your thoughts. I want to listen to your voice all the time and talk to you all the time. It's a yes from my side. It's all on you now, whatever you want. You can deny me but always remember, that someone is breathing only because you are, even after decades ...And once, my breath has stopped before yours. My breath will ask God to give it another chance so that it can continue to be with yours...

Subham was speechless. His eyes spoke through his tears instead. He hugged her and said, 'You are mine and will be mine till anyone breathes in this universe.'

Subham's mobile beeped...he looked. Ohh my result declared....

Sandhya exclaimed ...open it

He said I can't ...please do it

Sandhya opened the site and viewed the results...

She appeared disappointed

Subham understand things by looking at her face, and felt deeply disappointed as he failed too many expectations...

Sandhya hugged him...

Told him you can't always come top, but rank 2 is also satisfactory

Subham breakdown into tears and lifted Sandhya... I did it, now I will come back...yes...yes, and yes...both looked each other...mopped tears ...Subham told... I always thought that "will you ever realise" the depth of my emotions...

But you proved...emotions are everywhere, only thing that differs is the way of expression...

9 789356 282704

Printed by Libri Plureos GmbH in Hamburg,
Germany